True Life Survival

Contents

When disaster strikes ...   2

Sailing solo   4

The man who rode thunder   14

Tsunami!   22

Glossary   28

Index   29

Written by Janice Vale

Illustrated by Spike Wademan

Quiz No 213072
True Life Survival

Vale, Janice
B.L.: 3.9
Points: 0.5   MY

When disaster strikes ...

You've planned everything well. You're having a good time. Then, suddenly, something totally unexpected happens and your life is in danger.

You have to think fast and make decisions. Will you panic? Will you be able to get out of danger and survive?

In this book, three people face unexpected disasters and have to act quickly in an emergency.

A sailor, crossing the Atlantic Ocean, wakes to find he's in terrible danger. What will he do?

An aeroplane gets into trouble when flying at 14,600 metres. What will happen to the pilot?

And during a family holiday, a 10-year-old girl's life is thrown into danger when she sees the sea begin to bubble and foam …

Each of the three stories in this book really happened. Read them and think how you would cope if an unexpected emergency happened to you.

Sailing solo

Steven Callahan started sailing when he was 12. He had always wanted to sail **solo** across the Atlantic Ocean. When he was 30 years old, and an experienced sailor, he built a 6.4 metre-long boat called *Napoleon Solo*, which he raced in Europe.

He decided to sail back home to America from the Canary Islands across the Atlantic Ocean – a journey he thought would take five weeks, but it actually took a lot longer …

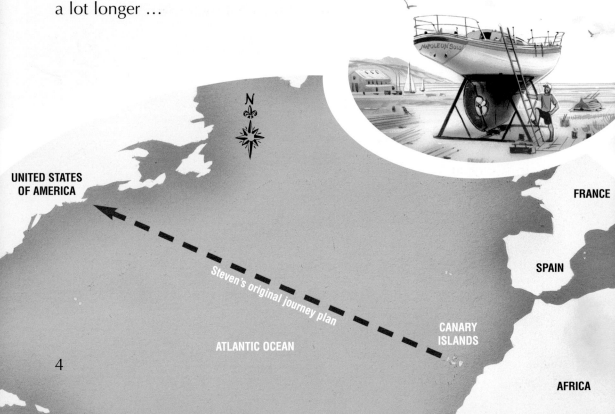

N

UNITED STATES
OF AMERICA

FRANCE

SPAIN

Steven's original journey plan

CANARY
ISLANDS

ATLANTIC OCEAN

4

AFRICA

Disaster!

For the first couple of weeks the sea was calm. Steven had plenty of food and drink, and he was looking forward to celebrating his birthday at sea.

Then, one night, his boat hit something and water poured in. Steven had just a few minutes to save himself from drowning.

He threw the heavy life raft into the sea. He dived under the rising water in his boat to grab what he could. He had his knife, his sleeping bag, an emergency pack, an empty can – and a cabbage. Then, with his knife clenched between his teeth, he jumped into the raft.

Napoleon Solo sank. Steven was alone, in a tiny raft, in complete darkness, in the middle of the ocean.

Alone in the ocean

Steven had no clothes with him because when the **collision** had happened he'd been in bed. The bottom of the rubber life raft was so thin it rippled like the sea beneath it.

He had a pump in the life raft, so he could keep refilling it with air. He had containers to catch fresh water in and a spear to catch fish. Would that be enough to keep him alive?

For the first week Steven huddled in his wet sleeping bag. His skin became covered in sores caused by the salt in the sea water and from lying on the wet rubber. His hands were raw from using the air pump. He ate the cabbage and dreamt of cakes.

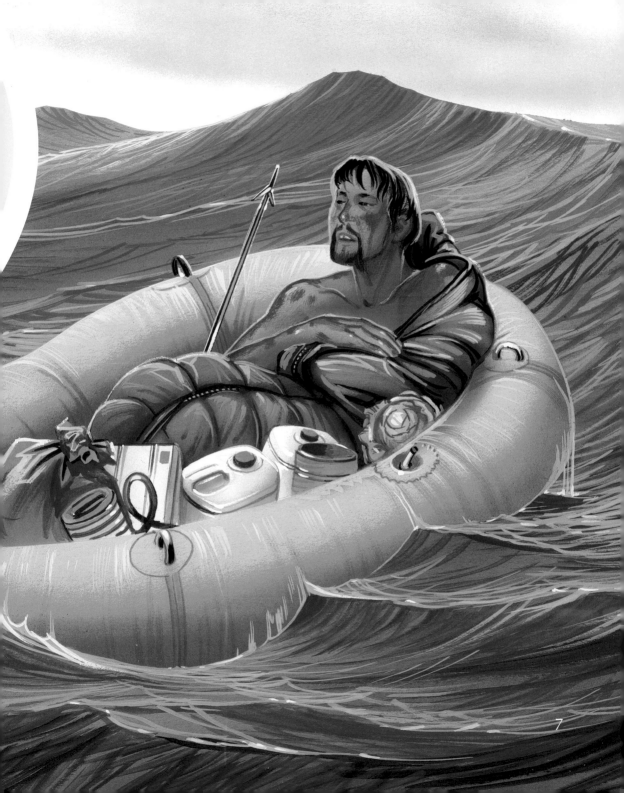

Sinking!

The raft drifted **westward**. Steven couldn't control its direction.

Then one day he realised the raft was deflating and folding up. Air was leaking out of it!

He scrambled for the patching kit instructions. They read: "Make sure raft is dry before gluing"! Steven spent days trying to make a patch stick over the hole and **bailing** water out of the raft. He was determined to survive.

After eleven days he managed to spear a fish, but he was too weak to pull it into the raft. Steven didn't give up. He got better at spearing fish and got used to eating them raw.

Shark attack

One day he saw a long, black shape in the water. A shark!
"What if it takes a bite out of the raft?" Steven thought. It went
round and round the raft, and there was nothing Steven could do.
He watched it, terrified. The shark finally swam away.

Rescue me!

Several times he saw ships' lights a long way off. He fired off a **flare**. But the ships didn't see him. He drifted for weeks and weeks. Sometimes huge waves poured into the raft and everything got soaked.

Steven allowed himself to drink one mouthful of his fresh water supply every six hours. His tongue swelled up in his mouth. On Day 17 and Day 58 it rained and he collected some of the rain water in a plastic box. By Day 70, he felt he couldn't go on any longer.

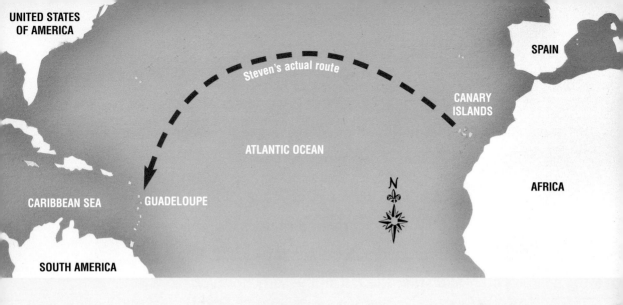

On Day 75 he saw a light. A ship? No. A lighthouse! That meant land! Steven drank a litre of his precious saved water. Three men in a fishing boat spotted him and gave him some coconut and sugar to eat. They took him to their island, Guadeloupe. Steven had drifted in his tiny liferaft, right across the Atlantic Ocean!

On dry land

When he got out of the fishing boat after nearly eleven weeks at sea, the soft sand felt like concrete because it wasn't moving up and down like the sea Steven was so used to. He had to be carried to hospital.

His family arrived by aeroplane to meet him and he gradually got better. When he was fully recovered he went sailing again. Steven invented a more efficient liferaft that had a sail, so that you could **steer** the raft in the direction you wanted it to go. Never again did he want to be adrift and at the mercy of the ocean's currents.

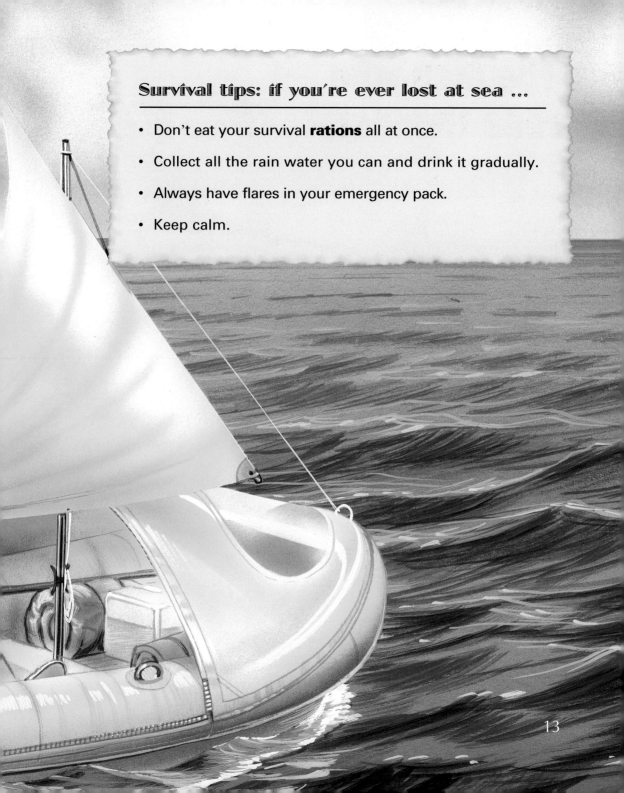

Survival tips: if you're ever lost at sea ...

- Don't eat your survival **rations** all at once.

- Collect all the rain water you can and drink it gradually.

- Always have flares in your emergency pack.

- Keep calm.

The man who rode thunder

Lieutenant Colonel William H. Rankin was an American Marine pilot. One day, he was flying his F8U Crusader aircraft at 14,600 metres. That didn't worry William. It was all part of his job testing fighter planes. But that day was different – his aeroplane's engine and radio suddenly stopped working.

If he stayed in the aeroplane he'd die. If he pressed the **eject** button, what would happen? No one had ever ejected from an aeroplane so high up before and survived, but it was worth the risk. He pressed eject and shot up out of the aeroplane.

Under pressure

At this **altitude** the cold air hit William instantly. It was unbearable. His hands froze numb. The different air pressure caused his body great pain. His eyes felt as though they were being ripped out. His head felt like it was splitting, and his ears felt like they were bursting. William's face and stomach **swelled** like balloons. He was bleeding from his eyes, ears, nose and mouth.

William cartwheeled down and down. His arms and legs were flung out wide. He kept trying to pull an arm in so he could hold the oxygen mask up to his nose. Eventually he managed to do it.

After a long time falling through the sky, he felt a massive jerk that nearly pulled him in half. It was his parachute opening at 3,000 metres, just as it had been designed to do.

"Soon I'll be on the ground," he thought.

Into the storm

But William had fallen into a thunderstorm. It hurled him back up
and up. The roar of thunder rattled every bone in his body and he
thought his teeth would fall out. He was in agony. The lightning
was too bright to bear, even with his eyes shut, and the wind
punched him breathless.

At one point, he opened his blood-filled eyes and was looking right
through a black tunnel in the cloud. Then he was squeezed into the
tunnel. He thought he would die.

Would the parachute last? What if it turned inside out?
Or caught on fire? Was he falling down or
being pushed up? William didn't know.

More trouble!

Then rain fell. It was so heavy William thought he was drowning.
He thought things couldn't get any worse, but they did.
Hailstones, as big as tennis balls, suddenly pounded him like hammers.

"I can't take any more," he thought.

Just then, 40 minutes after he had ejected from the aeroplane, the
rain became softer and the wind slowed down. The clouds parted
and William saw the most wonderful colour – green. It was land!

William looked down, trying to get another glimpse of that magic colour. There! Another rush of green! He braced himself for the landing … and fell into a tree.

He was back on Earth. William was battered, bruised and exhausted, but nowhere had ever felt more comfortable.

Tsunami!

The 2004 Christmas holiday was unusual for Tilly Smith. She and her family were staying at a hotel in Phuket in Southern Thailand. Instead of snow and cold, they were enjoying sun, sand and swimming. Tilly didn't know just how unusual her Christmas holiday was going to be until the sea "started to go funny" on December 26th.

On that day, while most of her friends from Danes Hill School shivered back in Oxshott in England, Tilly played on the beach in Phuket. She wasn't thinking about her home, her friends or school.

The blue sea started sloshing around at the shore and each incoming wave had a big froth on it. Tilly looked at this and then she looked out to sea. There were unusual swirls in the water, like little **whirlpools**, and the water turned more brown than blue.

It reminded Tilly of something. What was it? She remembered a video her teacher had shown the class of a **tsunami** that had hit the island of Hawaii in the Pacific Ocean.

Wave warning

"Look," Tilly cried. "I think it's a tsunami!"

No one took any notice. They didn't know what a tsunami was.

What they didn't realise was that a massive **earthquake** had happened in the ocean off the coast of northern Sumatra in Indonesia that morning and a huge amount of water in the ocean had started to move. Big waves were travelling fast across the Indian Ocean.

On the beach at Phuket, small waves swept up the beach, each higher than the one before it. The sea was creeping closer and closer to houses, hotels and shops. No one took any notice, except Tilly.

"It's a tsunami," Tilly yelled. "A tidal wave. It could come any second." She began shouting. "Get away. Run!"

People looked up from their beach games and sandcastles.

"Who is this crazy kid?" they thought.

"Hurry! Quick! TIDAL WAVE!" Tilly ran up and down the beach, screaming at people.

THAILAND

Phuket

Where the
earthquake
happened

INDIAN OCEAN

SUMATRA

INDONESIA

N

25

Run!

The water was now being sucked back from the beach and fish flipped about on the sand. People started to go down to the shore to watch what was happening.

"Don't go down there!" Tilly yelled.

"I know what this is!" she said. "We did it at school with Mr Kearney, my geography teacher. He taught us about earthquakes and tsunamis that happen after earthquakes. We have to go. Now!"

Tilly's dad hurried Tilly and her sister away from the beach. Tilly made sure everyone else on the beach was following them. Her mother, Penny, looked back at the sea. Suddenly it seemed to rise up and everyone ran.

The Smith family got to their hotel, which was built well back from the beach, just before the massive wave swept in. They climbed up to the third floor to escape the huge rush of water. The water crushed, smashed and destroyed everything in its path.

If anyone had been on that beach they would have been killed. But everyone had reacted to Tilly's warning and escaped just in time. The people on this beach were lucky. Thousands of other people died or were injured by the tsunami.

Survival tips: if you ever think you've spotted a tsunami ...

- Watch out for the danger signs, such as the tide going out quickly, whirlpools in the sea, and the water turning muddy.
- Get off the beach.
- Head for high ground.
- Stay with your family.
- Stay calm.

Glossary

altitude	the height above sea level
bailing	removing water from a container
collision	when something crashes into something else
earthquake	a violent vibration of the Earth's surface
eject	to force out
flare	a very bright signal light that can be fired into the sky
rations	very basic supplies such as food
solo	by oneself, alone
steer	to make something move in a particular direction
swelled	increased in size
tsunami	a giant wave caused by an earthquake under water
westward	towards the west
whirlpools	strong currents of water that move in circles

Index

aeroplane   3, 12, 14, 15, 20, 31

air pressure   16

altitude   16

Atlantic Ocean   2, 4, 11, 30

boat   4, 5, 11, 12, 30

currents   12

danger   2

earthquake   24, 26

emergency   2, 3

emergency pack   5, 13, 30

fish   6, 8, 26

flares   10, 13, 30

hailstones   20

Indian Ocean   24

land   11, 20

liferaft   5, 6, 7, 9, 11, 12, 30

parachute   17, 18

rain   10, 20, 31

sea   3, 22, 23, 24, 26, 27, 31

shark   9

survival rations   13, 30

thunder   14, 18

tsunami   22, 23, 24, 26, 27, 31

waves   10, 23, 24, 27

whirlpools   23, 27, 31

True Life Survival

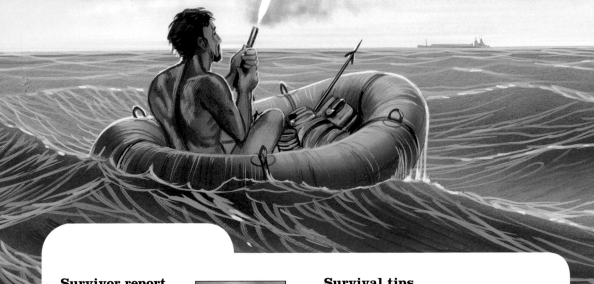

Survivor report

Steven Callahan

Event:

His boat sank in the Atlantic Ocean.

Action

He launched the life raft and grabbed his emergency pack, a knife, an empty can, a sleeping bag and a cabbage.

Survival tips

- Don't eat your survival rations all at once.

- Collect all the rain water you can and drink it gradually.

- Always have flares in your emergency pack.

- Keep calm.

Survivor report

Lieutenant Colonel William H. Rankin

Event:

His aeroplane's engine and radio stopped working when he was flying at 14,600 metres.

Action

He ejected from the aeroplane and fell through a thunderstorm.

Survival tips

- Keep calm.
- Choose your best option and act on it.
- Never give up.

Survivor report

Tilly Smith

Event:

She noticed a tsunami was going to hit the beach where she and her family were on holiday.

Action

She shouted a warning to everyone on the beach to get back from the sea.

Survival tips

- Watch out for the danger signs, such as the tide going out quickly, whirlpools in the sea and the water turning muddy.
- Get off the beach.
- Head for high ground.
- Stay with your family.
- Keep calm.

Ideas for guided reading

Learning objectives: appraise a non fiction book for its contents and usefulness by scanning, e.g. headings, contents list; identify how and why paragraphs are used to organise and sequence information; collect information from a variety of sources and present in one simple format; recreate roles showing how behaviour can be interpreted from different viewpoints

Curriculum links: Citizenship: developing a healthy, safer lifestyle; recognise the different risks in different situations and then decide how to behave responsibly

Interest words: altitude, atmosphere, bailing, emergency, Guadeloupe, hurled, tsunami, whirlpools

Resources: small whiteboard

Getting started

This book can be read over two or more guided reading sessions.

- Ask the children about any survival stories they know and encourage them to retell them in a dramatic and interesting way.
- Introduce the book by reading the covers and asking the children if they know anything already of the three stories and where they found the information.
- Quickly scan through the glossary to make sure they are familiar with the words and meanings.
- Demonstrate reading pp2-3 with appropriate expression and intonation. Decide why the paragraphs have been organised in the way they have. Stress that paragraphing helps reading aloud and builds atmosphere.

Reading and responding

- Encourage the children in pairs to choose and read one story each.
- Observe, prompt and praise the children reading, intervening to help with difficult vocabulary.
- Encourage the children to read aloud to each other, taking careful note of paragraphing to help with expression.
- Appraise the book together using key questions: *Is it interesting?*